™

The Whistle Pig

Duck Miller

Canvasback
Press

Published by Canvasback Press, Upperco, MD.

Although the author, editors, publisher, and book designer have used care and diligence in the preparation of this book and have made every effort to ensure the accuracy and completeness of the technical writing within, we assume no reponsibility for errors, inaccuracies, omissions, or any inconsistency herein. Names of places and people herein are fic-titious and any resemblance to any place or to any person, living or dead, is unintentional and coincidental.

The image of The Whistle Pig is a trademark of Canvasback Press.

Cover and interior design by Pneuma Books, LLC.
Visit www.pneumabooks.com for more information.

Publisher's Cataloging-in-Publication
(Provided by Quality Books, Inc.)

Miller, Duck.
    The whistle pig / Duck Miller. -- 1st ed. --
    p. cm.
    LCCN 2003100653
    ISBN 0972825606

    1. United States--Fiction. 2. Short Stories.
I. Title.

PS3613.I536W45 2004   813'.6
                                  QBI33-1199

    11 10 09 08 07 06 05 03   6 5 4 3 2 1

Keep America Beautiful!

Dedicated to
Don Geronimo and Mike O'Meara
who always inspire me to do more

Table of Contents

*If there wasn't anything to find out,
it would be dull. Even trying
to find out and not finding out
is just as interesting as
trying to find out and finding out;
and I don't know but more so.*

~Samuel Clemens

Introduction:
The Hunt

The delightful stories of *The Whistle Pig* present a unique opportunity to participate in a search for lost treasure. That treasure is the process of successfully exploring all that is hidden within this collection. Every word, line, or paragraph could nudge you toward the greater goal. What is that goal? The discovery of a key — a unique and unmistakable key hidden on accessible public property within the borders of the United States. The value of the key's physical location can only be discovered by searching out and prizing the allusions and references embedded within the stories.

In the day of the mega-million dollar jackpot — the same age that will not even permit the mass sanctuary of the *Titanic* to remain peaceful — Duck Miller turns back the clock to a time when self-discovery through knowledge was a form of entertainment. The key has been in place since February 2, 2003, and the clues to this literary puzzle are now in your hands. I suspect the adventure of discovering Duck's key may pique your interest, but his literary treasure chest can only be unlocked with your intellect.

As you delve into Professor Miller's trove, the pieces will slowly materialize. Pay close attention and you will perceive the greater picture. But be vigilant! The pieces come in many forms and this puzzle does not publish the number of pieces within the box. Without steadfast rules and armed with only vague instructions, you will be forced to open your mind to accept any reference as possible guidance. Go ahead. Test your perseverance, knowledge, and ability and allow the silhouette of a common groundhog to be branded upon your consciousness.

Look for the shadow of the whistle pig on your daily path. Share his secrets with those you hold dear, but beware the bright red of herring. Then again, investigating a herring may prove just as valuable as locating a key. Happy hunting!

Canvasback Press

PENNSYL
Dunkirk
Salamanca
Carrollton
Olean
Wellsboro
Blossburg
Coudersport
Warren
Smethport
Corry
Cambridge
Centre V.
Titus V.
Mead V.
Shafer
Utica
Buena Vista
Shippen
Morris
Cameron
Marion
Ridgeway
St. Mary
Oil City
Franklin
Greenville
Mercer
Sharon
Clarion
Ringgo
Romage
Lock Haven
Snow Shoe
Bellefonte
New Castle
Kittaning
Tyrone
Butler
Indiana
Altoona
Beaver
Clinton
Freeport
Ebensburg
Hollidaysburg
Huntingdon
Economy
PITTSBURG
Blairs V.
Jefferson
Johnstown
St. Clair
Greensburg
Hopewell
Moody Run
Perryopolis
Bedford
Connells V.
Somerset
Connellsburg
Washington
Wheeling
Clarks V.
National Rd.
Mound V.
Waynesburg
Union
Smithfield
Salisbury
Green Castle
Cumberland
Frostburg
Martinsburg
HARPERS FERRY
Morgan T.
Fairmount
Kingwood
Romney
Martins V.
Middlebourne
Prunty T.
Clarksburg
Grafton
Philippa
Moorefield
Winchester
Manassas
Front Royal
West Union
Weston
Buckhannon
Woodstock
Beverly
Newmarket
Luray
Glen V.
Cowman
Suttons V.
Franklin
Culpepper C.H.
Cedar Mt.
Marshall
Repose
Harrisonburg
Staunton
HARLESTON
Somerville
Kanawha
Huntersville
Charlottesville
Waynesboro
Palmyra

_____ *Year of the* _____

Black Heart Cherry

We walked in the filtered sunlight of the midday forest. The woodland path was wide, permitting the hand-in-hand stroll. The path was actually an overgrown fire trail cut by the Department of Game and Resources. The trail was supposed to allow emergency equipment access to the local watershed in case of a fire or other disaster. In reality, the path was primarily used by weekend fishermen or kids seeking some freedom from the rules or abuses of home.

The breeze kept the leaves high in the

treetops moving ever so slightly, and the result was not only refreshing but beautiful on the forest floor. It reminded me of the Latin term *Lux Nova*, which I learned in a theological lecture. The term is used to describe the divine colored shadows made from the sun passing though cathedral windows. Its remembrance made me glad to be outside and not trapped on the dark side of the stained glass.

Diane was pretending to enjoy the afternoon as much as I was, but I knew better. Not that she wasn't having a good time; she just did not have the same appreciation for a walk in the woods as I do. Well bred, better proportioned, and from a good-enough family, Diane grew up in the nice part of the city not far from the prep schools. She was born smart and cultured by education, social functions in New York, summers in Nantucket, and winter holidays at resorts out West.

Dark brown hair, thin, and the right height, she probably would have pursued modeling if her family had been a little less fortunate. A lot less fortunate and she may have sought to become a fortunate spouse. But my speculations were wild, even when founded, and I tried to forget the nonsense I had created by simply admiring her good looks. She was attractive and I wanted the afternoon to last.

We walked through a grove of pines and then downhill through a section of oaks mixed with poplars. As the fauna changed I scoured the ground for the corresponding fungi. It was late June and the little golden chanterelles were due to flush. Wild mushrooms are more fickle, less predictable, and much harder to find than women. One year the decaying wood produces a lush, plentiful crop and the next year nothing.

I generally did not talk too much about mushrooms and said nothing to Diane. It was a difficult topic to fully explain, and a little specific information might send her off plucking every Amanita in the woods inquiring, "How about this one?"

If the topic was brought up socially, it was usually because a friend was trying to verbally relive a college 'shroom experience which had only started after boozing all day at a football game. Not pleasant. In general, mushrooms are not a good topic of conversation. Most people who do know fungi are limited to that topic exclusively and exhaust my patience with a dozen stories all starting with, "One time I..."

If I could locate the precious edible treasure, I would verbalize the find, but until then it was better to stroll silently and let Diane initiate conversation she might enjoy. We had not yet been intimate but all was going well. Her body language let me know it would be okay. Well, the fact she even agreed on the afternoon was enough to know. Four years of higher education had taught me that once a woman has made physical contact — no matter how incidental — it would be okay. The smallest bump, brush, or misstep and you knew. I wish I had made this discovery in high school — but prep school girls are very different.

I almost met Diane ten years before when I accompanied a friend to a birthday cele-bration at a city country club. It was one of those outside evening gatherings where girls in summer dresses coveyed in small groups in the center of the party. The boys, decked out in loose-fitting khaki pants and blue blazers, marauded the outskirts, where the party lights abruptly stopped and the night began. As the evening progressed the male satellites were slowly pulled closer to the center of the party, losing some strength and gaining courage as they entered the brighter atmosphere.

I had spent most of the day of that party on a hay wagon twenty-two miles north of the city, methodically stacking hay with a man twice my age who had brown teeth. We'd worked side-by-side unloading each wagon, dust turning to grime as it stuck to our wet bare backs. In between heavy breaths, our conversation bounced with short blurbs about women, farming, and beer. He did not know anything about me, other than my ability to keep pace with him, and he was not apprehensive about being himself. Besides, I was just a kid.

Four hours later, I was well camouflaged in a white oxford with a cerise tie, and mixed in with those who were not particularly interested in hay wagons. The conversation, however, was similar, minus the farming part. Talk of college admissions and their father's business successes filled the void between women and beer.

I came with Townsand Banks. He was the only son of a commercial construction giant and better than most about not being a prick. He knew a little about the world and said he did not care about what women thought of him. I liked him because he was real. He understood the end game and respected me when it mattered.

After milling around for a couple hours, listening to mini-lectures on how the Ivy Leagues select their student bodies, I spotted the carnations and red roses. What a mesmerizing site. After I took a good long look I made my way back over to T.

"Why have I never seen the girl in the flowered dress?"

Townsand responded, "Probably hay dust in your eyes. I thought you farm boys were cunningly observant like foxes? She's always here unless she's out of town."

"Well I don't remember seeing her."

"How could you miss her? I guess I'll have to include you more frequently if you plan on sporting the game of the big town."

"Cut it out, Townsand," I said. "The big game goes down just like the lesser ones; you just have to use a bigger gun and stalk a little more. Do you even have a gun? What's her name?"

Townsand teased, "It's on the tip of my tongue and I just can't get it out."

It made for an interesting upbringing, jumping from the farmer's hay wagon and landing at a club of the privileged. With no help from Townsand, my plan to meet the girl in the flowered dress was never launched. It was getting late and the kids whose parents were out for the evening or gone for the month were headed home to consume what booze was available and then pass out — or consume each other.

"She's gone." Townsand said smugly. "You missed."

"I never fired."

"You're not kidding. Your city slicker buddy dresses you up, straightens your tie, gives you a shot to ease the edge frequently generated by the presence of the affluent, and what do you do? Nothing! Damn, it's hard to take the country out of the boy."

"Listen, Townsand. I didn't see you doing much but secretly nipping on that bottle you said you left in the car. Hiding your drinking is a clear sign of trouble to come. You could have at least dumped it in your soda. Is there any left?"

"No!"

"Bullshit. You've always got something."

"There is iced beer in the car but I am saving it for later. Have some patience."

"That's easy to say when you're already half flagged. What's later? I'm going to piss. Meet you by the car. Don't stumble in front of the manager on your way out — he'll call your mom. I think he has her number on the back of a matchbook."

I went to piss and lose the tie. I entered the club building from the patio door. The inside of the lower level of the club was as you might expect: dark wood, some blue hair, and old money drinking and smoking. Sometimes they looked up from their drinks as I passed. It was an uncomfortable feeling. It was a nonchalant, yet blank hateful look. Years later I realized their stares were not just for me but directed toward all youth.

I had forgotten the bathroom was equipped with an old black man. He was stationed to provide any service I could possibly need, as long as the help was a towel or proper shoe presentation. I wondered if there was an old black man in the women's loo. I pissed and decided to leave the tie on for awhile. I washed my hands and politely said thank you to the groom when he handed me a towel. His name tag read "Les."

I was now ready to dent Townsand's iced stash and make something good of the evening. I came through the restroom gate with too much steam and almost slammed the girl in the flowered dress. She had just left the women's restroom and also appeared to be headed for the valet line. She wasn't gone! I tried to think quickly.

I said excuse me and allowed her to pass first. I didn't have much time — less than two minutes. There were only about twenty-one or twenty-two gray marble treads to the top with one landing between. Once at the top, it was by the coat room and out the door. She was three treads ahead and although my position provided a wonderful viewing angle, I didn't have a next move.

I slowed my natural pace to stay three treads behind. My mind was blanking and inundated at the same time. I focused on the pattern of white carnations and red roses on her dress. Her beautiful hair blanketed her shoulders and draped the pattern on her silk dress perfectly. Was I star-struck? I could pull up beside her on the landing, but I didn't even know her name and I didn't know where T was taking us, nor if I could extend an invitation.

She kept the same pace. Did she know I wanted to say something more? Did she want to say something to me? She navigated the landing turn without looking back. For a fraction of a second, her right knee was not six inches from my right ear. As I made the turn, still three steps behind, I heard the din of a boisterous crowd from above. The main hall was located behind the circular lobby and it sounded as if a huge celebration was occurring there. I could hear a muted announcer speaking steadily but the crowd's roar did not seem to pause for him.

I saw the opportunity fading quickly. The circular lobby would be full of familiar faces, and surely someone would be quick to engage her with one last goodbye. She was at the top. She took two more steps before turning her head ever so slightly. I was still half a riser from the lobby level and did not have the best angle for viewing her eyes and lips.

The coat room attendant to our right could see it all. For twenty years Ms. Mary had politely received and returned the coats of the city's elite. She had a $5.50-per-hour box seat at the finish line. She had witnessed the formal beginnings and sloppy endings of all the great society events. Mary, the omniscient, was a lobby fixture, and that night was no different.

Ms. Mary could see the outcome of my pursuit. She witnessed the Smith girl break the plane of the top step before me. She was watching as the girl's head turned slightly and tilted. She saw me trailing behind hoping for some sort of interaction. I am sure Ms. Mary saw what I could not.

Ten years later Diane Smith was still every bit as stunning as she was on our first near-encounter at the country club. However, something had changed for me. The carnations and roses had long since been donated, and the excitement of the youthful awkwardness was gone. Besides, the tables had turned. Now she wanted me. The afternoon walk was progressing well enough, but I felt stuck searching the past.

"Would you like to find a nice spot to sit? I have a little snack in my sack and one big cold bottle," I propositioned Diane.

"Sure. Let's get closer to the water. What did you bring for us?"

"You pick the spot and I'll show you."

Diane led me off the trail and down to the water's edge. She picked a large flat rock that protruded out into the lake. A tall wild cherry tree shaded half the rock and it made for a good place to picnic in or out of the sun. The black cherries were ready to eat but were way out of reach. A few too ripe to hold on lay hidden in the short grasses beside the rock. Up the rise from our chosen dining rock a chestnut tree was in full bloom. That was always interesting, but Diane hadn't noticed yet. She immediately knocked off her shoes and submerged her feet in the water.

Diane asked, "Should we swim before or after we eat?"

"Before," I said. "You are aware that swimming in the watershed is prohibited? Are you good enough to make the far side and come back without trouble?"

As I turned to receive her response, the water splashed. I was strong in the water and could give her plenty of distance. I took my time and let her hit midlake before making a shallow dive.

After the swim, we ate while still dripping and lay in the sun to dry and rest.

{DM}

Grandfather's Office

Once inside the barn, with the door secure and my eyes closed, my ears waited for Grandfather to initiate the sharp snap of the old switch that would burn the evenly spaced bare electric bulbs. The bulbs lined the center of the main hall's ceiling, and as neat and clean as the barn was kept, those bare bulbs were always filthy. I think it was the bulbs that kept my grandmother out. Spotted with bug dirt, hay dust, and the patterns of burned moths, those bulbs were ugly before they were lit. Once powered, the light they produced was hard on the morning eye. We could turn them off after an hour or so, but by then it did not matter because the progress of day had already bleached their potency away.

The morning barn appeared just as it had been left the night before. All the tools of our trade were stored in their proper places. The hoses were perfectly coiled beneath the spigots, feed and straw were walled vertically as if a mason had struck a line and dropped a plumb, and the buckets were stacked with drying towels draped squarely on top. It was a good feeling to start the day with such a clean slate.

Grandfather's office was at the far end of the great hall — opposite the door we had entered. It was a large wooden barn, and the course down to the office was a greater distance than it appeared. The trip to the office provided a good opportunity to review the state of the operation, and Grandfather reminded me of a general inspecting his men as he walked.

With the morning news and other paper

forms trapped under his arm, Grandfather and I traveled side-by-side toward the office door. The sound from our shoes on the asphalt floor echoed slightly in the morning silence. Grandfather's gait was long and stronger than most of his age. For every five of his paces, I required six to keep up. Unlike my father and mother, he never broke his stride for my benefit. I understood that I was responsible for covering the same ground in the same time if I wanted to stand ahead of his shadow.

That simple trip from the entry to the office door was always invigorating. The smell of the barn, the sound of our shoes, and our ultimate destination made me feel strong and glad that I could accompany my grandfather. Someday the hoses would be coiled and the feed stacked neatly at my command.

At the office door, Grandfather would always look back down the hall before glancing at the charts and reviewing the information left by the help on the post board. There were pigeonholes to the left of the door. The holes organized time cards, schedules, and instructions. Names written in black marker on masking tape labeled the compartments. Grandfather was particular about removing the old tape if an existing name was replaced by a new one. Accumulating new tape on top of old tape was not his style. I was frequently reminded of how this sort of thing should be done.

The office door was unmarked and only fully closed at night. The door was split horizontally; the bottom had a small counter at its top. The lower door remained closed during the day, forcing the farm hands to lean over when addressing their boss.

We frequently saw visitors who did not know the location of the office timidly poking their heads through other doors on the main hall in what must have seemed a fruitless search. Eventually, our disoriented company would find someone to ask, but Grandfather and I secretly enjoyed counting just how many times a newcomer would peek into the wrong room before inquiring.

Looking through the top half, visitors could see the office was a rectangular room with wood plank flooring that ran the room's full length. At the far end of the room, surrounded by book shelves and centered on the wall, a single double-hung window permitted the morning sun to cast long rays on the opposite wall.

The shelves carried a great weight of books and periodicals — some very old. Entire sections of shelving were dedicated to Grandfather's fascination with the heroes of history and fiction. Many authors appeared more than once in the collection. Topics that only deserved a single entry, with titles like *Pythagorean Numerology in the Modern Day*, *Successful Orienteering*, and *Hunting and Fishing with Ernie*, acted as dividers and separated the larger, more established sections of the collection.

One entire shelf — four feet in length — was dedicated to the Age of Discovery. On numerous occasions Grandfather lectured me on the routes traveled and perils faced by those who founded our great country. The rhythm and voice of his lecture style always reminded me of Charlton Heston as

Moses; he sounded like someone you should listen to.

He would begin, "Spurred and then driven by some irresistible desire to trail the setting sun in vehicles that amounted to nothing more than skiffs, the worthy left the safety of the familiar ground of their birthplace and took their chances on the mercy of the North Sea. Many died just shy of the ultimate goal... fading behind the blurring gray sea with no one to witness the sight or mourn the loss. Others were failed by the ineptitude of their navigators and nights too dark to see stars. Some just bumped into a little bad luck and never recovered. But those who were the first, chosen not by God but by determination, were permitted to seed their triumphant nature..."

As Grandfather narrated, I preferred to study the mapped routes and read the accounts of those who did succeed. History is not so kind to those who just try — those names are almost always lost. The vividness of Grandfather's lectures was an interesting gift. Of course, he didn't take on the North

Sea in an open boat, nor did he have to trust a crude sexton to blaze his life's path, but he spoke as all great orators do — as if he were part of the discovery.

To the left of the bookshelves, a heavy wooden table buttressed the northern wall of the office. Grandfather used the table as a desk. It was accompanied by a burgundy leather swivel-chair with three brass rollers. After years of use, the chair's rollers had worn circular and oval swirls in the wooden floor. When I swept the office, dust would always remain in scratches beneath the chair, highlighting the rollers' wear.

Above the table was a calendar displaying a scenic picture of a rock formation at a drought-stricken reservoir. Little patches of multiflora rose and spring flowers grew out of rock crevices in the picture. In a wet year, the rocks would have been submerged and not worthy of the photographer's time. The picture was taken in what grandfather called "the post card tradition" — although interesting at first, it quickly became mundane and ordinary.

The grid part of the calendar had thirty-one boxes full of marks, x's, and handwritten annotations in various ink colors or pencil leads. In the last box of the first row, the second day of the month, there was a hand-drawn, five-pointed, black star. Unlike the other scribble, this symbol was small but predominant. The symbol, just like the little gold fish in the second box of the next line, was not repeated in Grandfather's calendar legend.

On the wall to the left of the table, a large plastic-coated map of the United States hung by three thumb tacks. A tack secured each of the top corners, while the third tack fastened the bottom right. I could not understand why Grandfather tolerated this, but he esteemed anyone who knew the wisdom of holding their tongue, so I never asked. Grandfather's map was unmarked. He preferred the country to appear unblemished — unlike his calendar.

My chair was placed to the right of the window. It was an old oak school chair and

not friendly to the seat. Grandfather said it
was that way for a reason.

{DM}

Two Dogs

The stone house sat in the center of the farm. Its covered wooden porch encircled the entire dwelling. Many generations of our family's children had run round and round that porch, playing games and making races. The house was big and the full trip circumnavigating the porch was pretty substantial for the smallest of relatives. A crawler or toddler making for the corner frequently sent mothers scurrying in hot pursuit. It seemed someone was always coming or going from a corner.

The Whistle Pig

That porch was the theater on which all family events unfolded. In the warmer months, breakfast, lunch, and dinner could be taken outside. Weddings, wakes, christenings, and the teenage mischief of summer nights provided everybody with porch memories of some sort. It was a good place to grow up.

An antique wooden radio on a stand was positioned against the stone wall among the Amish-built rockers and the gray gypsy wood porch furniture. The old radio was there for decoration and nostalgia, as modern sound had recently been piped into hidden speakers from a control board in the library. I often watched the men on the porch as I walked down the drive or played way out in the yard. The beginning of a radio broadcast of the baseball game would get the men to their feet in unison. After a motionless period they would all sit back down. I couldn't hear the radio far out in the field and the men appeared as if they were in church obeying an invisible pastor. It always looked funny from where I stood.

Two Dogs

One Saturday afternoon before a ball game broadcast, as the uncles and male cousins gathered in the cool shade of the summer porch, my father recited a story about the farm when he was my age. I sat directly in front of dad's white oak rocker on a retired three-legged milking stool. My uncles and older cousins semi-circled around us while most of the other younger children played in the dust.

"This is a story about two dogs that lived at opposite ends of the porch that we are sitting on right now. The dogs have long since died and are buried on the farm, but they lived their lives on and around this porch.

"Both beasts were male Labrador retrievers from the same litter. The one named Sam was a bright white-yellowish color and the dark one's name was Tom. Even though the dogs were from the same litter, I think their fathers might have been different, as that sometimes happens with dogs. We never talked about that with anyone outside the family, and, besides, the papers said otherwise.

"Tom was an uncommon critter, but very

steady, and he worked like a clock managing the farm. He kept the foxes out of the chicken yard, alerted the house when someone came down the drive, and retrieved whatever was necessary. He was trustworthy, powerful, and had a glossy black sheen to his coat. If he had ever been sold, he would have brought top dollar because he listened and knew how to please his owner. But he was not for sale, even though all the local sportsmen inquired. They would have paid a high price to have Tom work among their decoys, pursuing downed ducks in the winter marsh.

"Sam, who lived at the other end of the porch was primarily interested in defending his space near the kitchen door. He knew what door the bones came out of! He was not quite as loyal as Tom, but he acted when called on. Sam was the kind of dog that seemed a bit more concerned with his own situation than that of his owner. Don't get me wrong, he was a good dog, but he didn't take orders quite like Tom. Sam was born with an interesting natural independence that I have never seen in another canine. He was a fighter. He never backed down, always went strong and hard, and he never went anywhere without leaving a wake.

"Now from those descriptions you might think Tom was the choice of the two. But Sam excelled at things that Tom did not. Tom was always eager to please, and if he lacked ability he surely made up for it in laborious effort. Sam, on the other hand, found a way to get the less mundane feats accomplished. Dad took Tom hunting when he needed a retriever. Dad selected Sam when he needed a strategic partner to locate and flush a pheasant. The inherent differences of the two were beneficial for our family and the farm, but made for trouble between the dogs.

"As puppies the two dogs wrestled and growled in play. They also crashed into anything that could be knocked over. We kids loved it, but your grandmother didn't care for it one bit. She was always shooing them out into the yard. After the puppies grew into their feet they migrated to opposite ends of the porch and lived like distant relatives. On occasions when they simultaneously turned a corner and were forced to acknowledge each other face-to-face, the war would begin. Most of their fights lasted for rounds. It always started with the dogs rolling off the porch in a balling, bawling, brawling mess.

"The fighting was hard to listen to and wasn't fun to watch after the initial go. Just when it looked like the dogs were spent and ready to find neutral ground to lick their wounds, it would start again. Back and forth and back and forth until Sam was pink and turning red and Tom was near whipped crippled.

"After those big battles, the hounds would be banished from the porch. They were too bloody and beaten for proper display. The cool dirt and shade beneath the porch made recuperation more bearable no doubt. After a couple days both dogs would return topside and life would go on with no declared winner.

"Sam and Tom were also bulls. Farmers, waterfowlers, and interested Lab novices from the entire tri-state peninsula would bring their hot bitches for mating. Sam and

Tom fathered so many litters that Labs bred locally will always have some part of Sam and Tom's genes in their blood.

"Some who came to the farm for the service had grandiose illusions of what a breeding facility was supposed to be like. The first-timers were usually surprised. They often asked, 'Why do the dogs looked so banged up?' or 'How could you let such beautiful animals scar up their bodies?' or 'It's a shame the way you have permitted them to act!'

"It was mostly the people that thought they knew what was best for animals that had a problem. Not so much the animal lovers *per se* but the dog fanatics — the ones who view dogs as children or equal to people in some unnatural way. Farmers and sportsmen never questioned a scar or little cut. When accused about the condition of the dogs, your grandfather usually said, 'I think the sperm inside is okay.' I always waited for that. The expression of horror on the offended faces was so great. Most of those owners usually left without breeding their dogs. They were proud that they really loved and cared about their bitches unlike us and our boys. Then again, those pet owners never described a female dog as a bitch, but that's not what our story is about.

"The next big decision for the interested customer was which bull. Sometimes it came down to what dog was on the porch at the time. It was a scene worthy of a spot on the silver screen, when granddaddy looked up to the porch to see which dog was around. Casually he would say, 'Oh, Tom is off today. How about Sam' or vice-versa.

"Most didn't care which sire delivered the seed — being they were brothers — but the customers who thought they could predict the color of the puppies sometimes made arguments for their choice of studs. Dad would just say, 'Mostly black' and comment no farther."

The opening of the ballgame ended dad's story, and thinking of Tom and Sam, I ran out in the field to watch the men on the porch.

{DM}

Full Moon

The year was '63, the second day of July. It was well after midnight. The intense humidity and the present situation on the Eastern seaboard made the divine struggle tight. I had committed myself to discharging my duties honorably and sworn to uphold the law of the land. Hopefully, my actions could generate a greater comfort, if only events would come to pass as I desperately needed — then I could think straight and continue to guide the country with clarity.

I sweat the bed until I could no longer bear

the great weight I felt inside, and I headed out to pace the west garden. I had not felt right for some time. The late news of the day's engagement had left my stomach churned and its contents binding. It was difficult to depend on Meade, and tomorrow's actions might very well destroy my weakened constitution.

The west garden was not much cooler than the bedroom. I did feel a little better walking, but the need to regain the regularity of a peaceful nation was pressing. The evening telegraph accounts of the once golden Wheat Field, The Peach Orchard, and the countless damaged men with their innards full of only cherries, lead stones, or nothing at all haunted me to nausea.

The lifeblood of the greatest estuary in the world will surely run red — fouled by the run-off of the lives lost today. It would take both rivers and all of the streams in between to cleanse the watershed of the immense waste created by such violent troop movements.

If I could just move undaunted: above the smell of the field, above the vapors and toxic gases of the wasteland, above the bowels of hell, above the battlefield, I could precisely direct dropping the charged loads. Then I could bring a quicker resolve than Meade. I need to relieve this constant infection that has plagued me and the country. I must forcefully move.

I left the garden and walked unaccompanied down to the Potomac's edge. The security detail would be upset upon the discovery of my absence but I needed solitude. I descended to the water's edge and pressed my back firmly against the cool clay of the river's exposed bank. It was a good place to concentrate. I saw a river turtle duck his head back beneath the black water. The calming movement of the night river was perfect.

The reflection of the moon in the high water marked the space beneath me. Small ripples briefly animated the reflection and encouraged my spirit. I was determined to win this battle, then the war, and reunite the nation.

{DM}

Winter Land

Annie and I departed from New York on New Year's Day and planned on arriving in San Francisco before sundown Friday, February 22. That only gave us fifty-three days to cross the country. It sounds like a lot of time, but Annie was good at finding interesting places to stop and hang out. She's the type of person that wanders around a corner and instantly finds a new paradise, full of the best that life has to offer. She could hypnotize a new acquaintance, male or female, just by saying hello. People always want to be around her. I guess that's why I promised to keep my end of the deal and deliver her to the far coast.

I was apprehensive about stopping anywhere for more than a single day or night, because growing even the shortest of roots could postpone Annie's debut in California. I also had to consider the winter weather as I didn't want our fate to twist like that of George Donner's ship. A fool I was not — at least about the weather.

I tuned the radio to a station playing a folksy rambling song and we took off, leaving the apple spinning. Annie was in the back of the van, laying on top of a fuzzy crimson blanket in a new year's daze. The previous night's celebration had temporarily damaged, but not destroyed, her goods. She wore only an oversized green three-quarter sleeve football jersey with a white number 74 on the front and back. She still had some confetti ribbon woven into her brown hair. It was pretty much the same thing she'd worn the night before and, in fact, the same shirt she'd had on the night of her debut.

Although the ultimate goal was Annie's timely delivery to San Francisco, I had one stop of my own to make. The reason and location for my diversion was kind of a secret — the sort of information that if you ever told a single person you would regret it forever. I had once been entrusted by my friend Coop with such a secret. I think it was the only mistake he ever made. With some luck I could make my stop unbeknown to Annie and spend the rest of the trip following her free will and wanderings.

She woke up four hours closer to the Pacific and asked if we could eat. My cup had been empty for some time and I was ready for hot coffee. It had started snowing and I began looking for someplace to stop. I found just about the only place open and eased the van off the road. Annie was still only half dressed so I left her in a snug ball in the warmth of the van.

After waving to the old man sitting inside the storefront's frosty window pane, I picked up the gas pump. The attendant did not appear to acknowledge me, but the pump came to life. The snow was beginning to accumulate on the ghostly quiet country road and the vacant parking lot. Falling snow has a unique no-sound, you can and can't hear it. Annie called it a deafening silence. At that moment the area seemed too peaceful a place for people. I clicked the pump off and walked toward the store.

Inside Stephen's General Store the bearded old man was dropping a chunk into the top of his potbelly stove, to which his stomach bore some resemblance. He turned as I walked in but strangely did not look up. The place was poorly lit and it took my eyes seconds to adjust. There were a couple of stools at a lunch counter in the back, but the lights were off over the grill. To my dismay the only recognizable smells were smoke and coffee. Bacon and eggs would have been better, but it was New Year's Day and the cook was probably still asleep.

Always prepared, I gathered enough food stuffs for the next twenty-four hours — just in case other stores were closed or if we got snowbound. As I walked back to the front to pay for the gas, groceries, hot coffee, and a big mesh bag of oranges, I looked over the old man's shoulder, through the single frosted window pane, and watched the van pull out onto the snow-covered road. The man did not look up but reached out over the counter and felt for my hand.

{DM}

For the Record

Furry, brown, and oh so small
Our tunnels go deep below it all
We rise above to eat and meet
And return beneath to toil and sleep

Those above, they do not dare
To invade our presence here
But what jealous hearts they bare
When we do escape our fear

A high-pitched shriek stands me short
Ears alert, my eyes see long
I hear not the crack report
Shadow silent, sight is gone

Dusty dirt turns moist and black
As flies buzz, land, nibble 'round the back
Kin emerge to eat once more
Cycle repeats, as in days of yore

Cork

His name was Gerald Lee Winston, but most everybody called him Cork. We waited in uncomfortable red chairs at the station for the last bus to come from the city — but no Gerald. I was quietly disappointed and wondered if he was still alive. Ma did not say anything.

It started raining on the way home. There was a small rotten rusted hole on the passenger side floor of the old Chevy truck. It was a small puncture, but you could see the road if you looked down at the right angle.

The Whistle Pig

When the truck tire hit a puddle, little water droplets sometimes splashed in depending on its size and depth. It was a hard drive home with an empty seat and no explanation for Gerald, so I watched the rusted spot on the floor and estimated how many droplets would make it from the road below to the puddle inside.

Rick was the oldest. We still had his letters begging mom and dad to adopt kids he was going to try and send back stateside. We only got letters from Rick for about thirteen months. When they stopped, it was over. Those kind of letters never came from Gerald, although he frequently would mail us pictures and stuff that was different from anything we had at home.

In fact, the only thing his letters and packages had in common was that he never signed his name. Come to think of it, he really never wrote too many words. He would send whatever caught his eye with something circled or underlined. Our old dented black postbox became an international Cracker Jack box linking Appalachia to Southeast

Asia. We often raced barefoot out the lane to be the first to pry the tight-hinged door down to see what surprise Gerald had sent.

The longer he was gone the more abstract his mailings became. After a few particularly weird pieces arrived, one being an eighteen-inch, tightly-braided, black and gray ponytail, Dad got the mail.

Gerald did make it back, although no one had ever notified us that he would be twenty-eight days late. Dad was coming home from work in a late afternoon thunderstorm when he found Gerald just standing in the rain at the end of the drive by the postbox. Dad pulled the truck up and his second son got in as if he was a child waiting for the school bus. I don't know what they talked about or if they talked at all on the way down the drive, but we were all happy Gerald was home.

For the next year Gerald spent most of the daylight hours down by the railroad tracks by a wooden bridge you could sit under to get out of the sun. Cork would set up bottles on the tracks and wait for the iron horse to come and shatter the glass into dust. I went with him sometimes, but it was always the same. Line up the bottles and wait for the big train.

{DM}

Forty-Eight States

What an incredible country. I was having lunch under what little shade there was at a highway rest stop in the desert outside of Las Vegas. I was alone at a picnic table when a dusty private tour bus rolled in. The driver left the bus running and parked it away from the few cars stopped close to the restrooms and vending machines.

I could not see any activity through the coach's tinted windows, so I sat chewing fried chicken and wondering who might be inside. After some time, a short guy with long dark hair and a black shirt emerged from the bus. His brief appearance only seemed to confirm his previous prediction: yes, he was in the blistering-hot, super-bright desert. He turned tail and disappeared back into the cool air.

After I had finished another leg and started on a breast, the door opened again. This time an old, tattooed, shirtless man came out carrying two bottles of beer and a worn spiral notebook. As he walked toward me I could not help but notice the whiteness and age of his exposed skin. The green and reddish tattoos had become loose and less distinct, as gravity pulled hard at their faded color.

He offered me a beer and asked if he could sit down. I said yes and he capped the beer with a little opener he carried in the spiral part of the notebook. The handle of the bottle opener had a pen inside and appeared to be quiet handy. He sat down and handed the cold brown bottle to me.

"Shall we drink to the desert?" he suggested.

"Good enough," I replied.

I took the best drink of beer I have ever had, and it was only 11:30 in the morning.

"Thanks for the beer. It tastes pretty damn good... Well, are you 'the man' or are you part of the entourage?" I questioned.

He did not look up from his spiral notebook but replied, "Right now the entourage, but later when they start working, I will take the appearance of the man for a couple hours."

"Must be tough. That's a nice coach, but it can't be like home. Would you like some chicken? I bought it back in Vegas at a place with a little counter and no drive-through."

"Not now. Maybe after I'm finished."

I tried to be cool and relaxed about what was going on, but it was strange as hell. One minute I was alone eating fried chicken in the middle of the desert, and the next minute some crazy rock-'n-roller with multicolored beads strung in his eighteen-inch gray beard and rose-glass shades was sitting across the picnic table sharing a cold one with me while writing lyrics with a short pen equipped with a bottle opener at the other end.

I wish I knew this guy's name. Mysteriously, I missed the introduction part of this encounter. The rhinestones on his belt and boots and the coach delivery must make him somebody. The side of the bus was void of a name and looked brand new. I decided that it would be rude to ask and guessing would probably be a mistake.

He did not look up. He'd write some words, swallow some beer, and write some more words. Suddenly, his right arm, the arm with the hand holding the multipurpose pen, went up to full extension and then back down. I thought the dude was having some kind of epileptic fit. He still did not look up. A woman in a lacy black gypsy dress came out of the bus and brought two more bottles of beer. She sat them on the table, took the pen out of the artist's hand, opened the beers, and then pushed the pen part back between his fingers. She smiled at me, turned, and went back to the bus.

"Nice looking woman, isn't she?"

Not my style, but I said, "Sure."

Then the man raised his head from his work. He looked at me like I had chicken grease on my face. I felt strangely uncomfortable. His head was tilted and I thought he might just lie down and die right there or without notification shoot his hand back up in the air. Then he responded, "One of these songs once made an average guy real big for a while."

"Yeah, what's the story?"

He paused and looked back down to the page and said, "The guy was what I would call light sensitive." The artist quietly cleared his throat and gently rehearsed, "He woke up in the limelight, stumbled into the spotlight, burned in the bright, fired at the starlight, sought refuge in the bar light."

"I guess you are lucky and not bothered by the light?"

He smiled without moving his head and took another drink of beer.

{DM}

Sand Castle

We went to the shore twice each year, once in the late spring and again in the early fall. My sister, Ella, was two years older, so she naturally became the forewoman on all of our sand construction projects. Being the boy, I was responsible for the structural and grunt work of the site. Ella was responsible for shopping the beach for the necessary ornamentation, while I chose the ground worthy of our work. Before Ella started her stroll, she always provided instructions regarding the height, shape, and design of the project.

"Today, your name will be Mr. Silas. You will be the wealthy self-made man capable of attempting completion of such a structure. I am commissioning you to construct a great castle on this beach, a sand palace having size and beauty like one no other Boston beach-goer has attempted. Here are my require-ments: a shallow oval moat, a secret tunnel, walls surrounding the village, gardens and houses inside the walls, a wishing well, a grand palace with two spires, and a river feeding the moat.

"I will be responsible for the decoration. Don't you worry about shells and drift-wood. You just move sand. Begin! You have a deadline, you know. And please construct this grand palace to withstand the wind and surf. It must remain until we return in the fall!"

I guess birth order made me the whipping boy, but as long as I fulfilled Ella's list of re-quirements and didn't attempt decoration, I could create as I pleased. I always planned and plotted the tunnel first. It was most im-portant that the little sand crabs could enter easily and take refuge under my impressive structure. Ella thought I was building the palace solely for her to decorate with the grandeur of surf debris, but if you asked me when she was not around, it was mostly for the crabs.

The tunnel had to be started first because my arm would not be long enough to reach the center after the walls were completed. I would pre-dig the tunnel, aiming inland, so that the beach entrance would have the mass of the castle to protect it from the rising sea. After the village was completed the final touch would be mining the second leg of the tunnel eastward from the outside back toward the center to complete the passage.

Ella's order for spires was a surprise. If she was forced to move sand alone her creations were always low, circular, and empty in the center. On the other hand, I loved to master the tall tower and walls. My castles needed to rise up and alter the flatness of the barren beach shore. Obtaining the desired height depended on the width of the base and the wetness of the sand. The wetter the sand, the harder it packed and the more impressively my towers soared.

By the time the excavation and formation was nearly complete, the princess Ella returned with her weighted plastic pail. She would line shells, worn stones, smoothed wood, and other products of the lapping tide in perfectly neat rows beside my structure. It was always the same. After Ella emptied and categorized her bucket, she instructed me to leave my castle and fill the voids in her collection.

"We are short twelve rounded black stones, twenty-one small scallop-shaped shells, and four feet of this stuff that looks like it should be around a hula dancer's neck. Oh, and five more pebbles that look like pearls. Those spires are too thin and tall. Make them shorter, fatter, and closer together when you get back," Ella said.

In my eyes, the castle was perfectly good the way it was — undecorated. I never minded a little sprucing up, but Ella needed to add feminine touches as if directed by a stronger force. Even as a young boy I feared what I would later realize as the evils of stewartship — a powerful force that can cause independence to hibernate, replacing the beauty of diversity with a single cookie cutter. Ella had already been infected by the age of thirteen and was trying to make me a slave too.

Regardless, I went out toting the purple plastic pail to locate the missing pieces that Miss Ella desired but could not find. Dad was sitting in an upright beach chair in his customary spot, reading a magazine and eating red pistachios. There must have been fifty red shells that could have been incorporated beautifully into the grandeur of the sand palace, but I knew better than to try to substitute any item on the list.

I scavenged the beach until I was too far away to see where I had started. The pail contained only a portion of Ella's list, but I was hungry and ready for lunch. On my way back I found twelve more inches of the stuff that looked like hula dancer neckwear. It smelled so bad I wanted to pretend I never saw it, but Ella would be happy. An empty stomach really magnifies the stench of decaying sea life.

As I approached the sand castle I saw a crab scurry sideways away from a sea gull and into the tunnel entrance. Ella and Dad had already gone up to the house.

{DM}

Egg Hunt

I was born in April 1923. It became a family tradition that my birthday celebrations were organized around the most expansive egg hunts that my parents could possibly host. Neighbors, relatives, and friends came prior to dawn to take part in the event. Rain or shine we set out to scour the countryside with our eager eagle eyes and baskets full of refreshments to fortify us for the long day.

As I grew older the event became more challenging and its following much more serious. It was not anything like the toddler stumbles that local churches and communities conduct. Those hunts are based on pleasing all with the reward of full baskets. The run and grab of church events was not a premise that my father followed in his preparation and planning for our hunt. He was a painter and a historian and cherished quality over wealth.

His commitment to the day made our event well known to everyone in the area. Only thirteen highly crafted eggs were placed for discovery. Dad painted each egg as if it were an oval canvas commissioned by royalty. Twelve of the eggs would always share that year's theme. Dad drew his yearly themes from all that he thought had value. Great American paintings, state flowers, famous personalities, and even members of a world championship baseball team all had their year to grace the eggs. Some years however, the theme was obvious only to my father.

The thirteenth egg was considered the most valuable and did not directly share the theme of the field. It received a more prestigious decoration. The finder of that treasure won the day. All the eggs possessed a corresponding number that were announced during the morning roll call. My father would address the participants — he called us the *pursuit* — at dawn. He would stand on a box in front of the gathered team and describe each painting on every egg in the field. He never described the thirteenth painting. That treasure was for the blessed to share at their discretion.

The eggs' ultimate locations were often linked to the colored oil on their shells. The finder frequently did not piece together the link between the oil pattern and its location until the prize was claimed, but on occasion my father's commencement description of each egg helped steer the thinking pursuit.

The only years the complete collection was reassembled for all of the pursuit and crowd to view were 1945 and 1956. Most years the thirteenth egg was never found, and along with other allusive members of the field, it was sacrificed back to the soil. It was an important part of the hunt to allow the unfound eggs to remain hidden. It seemed a terrible waste of painstaking artistry but the loss of the unfound — according to Dad's theory — made the collected all the more cherished.

The event lasted the entire day, as our home bordered a park which allowed unlimited acreage for egg placement. Dad preferred to trail the pursuit out of the yard and into the hills at the beginning of day. He would return to the yard prior to any detections. Positioned close to his soap box, he would receive and congratulate those worthy of his eggs. His greatest joy was the eagerness of the pursuit at the outset of the day and then their exhausted return.

Although I found many eggs over the years, my favorite find was the thirteenth entry the year of the "firsts" theme. I found the egg incorporated neatly into an occupied wild turkey's nest among the brown leaves on the forest floor. The bird was peacefully sitting on her own eggs along with the thirteenth. More cherished than finding the egg was the vision father had applied to the shell. There was even a secondary

miniature rendition of Jack opposite the
egg's primary painting.

{DM}

The Bow

Brother Calvin was born during the sunniest downpour I have ever seen. A rain fell so hard and so fast that it puddled immediately on the ground. Raw, isolated, tightly-packed, greenish clouds dispersed their contents so locally that adjoining fields and woods did not even get wet. Everybody gathered for the labor went outside to witness the strange occurrence.

The sun was past the high point of its arched journey, at about a sixty degree angle in the western sky. Heavy bands formed as the light burned through the moving water. Everyone on the porch stood in awe at the sight.

Covering the entire valley, the arch rested its grounded points gently on each ridge. Rich bands of color announced the event on nature's billboard. Outstanding in its display, a photo of the storm and glowing lights would have looked fixed or doctored because it was too picturesque — near perfect. Substantial discussion and speculation of the event accompanied Cal through his entire impressive life. Should the birth arch be mentioned to him in passing, he would dispel the account as urban legend or happenstance.

Lacking a worthy explanation for the display, the proud members of the family just referred to the phenomenon as the day Calvin was born. Except for our mother and of course baby Calvin, we were all able to see the storm and the bow. A happy and joyous day of firsts it was. Virtually all of the valley's inhabitants eventually heard how our family gathered outside to stare up at the sky as the matriarch delivered new life inside the house. Everyone who heard the story wondered what would become of the boy whose birth was so splendidly announced.

"That which you cannot explain should not have a fixation on one's soul and surely should not be paid more attention to than other more practical topics," Cal often said. He was frequently questioned and urged to provide an explanation for his great accomplishments. Every reporter wanted to hear Cal praise something divine instead of his independent persistence and refined skill, but that did not happen.

Cal often mentioned the importance of staying focused, working hard, and the benefits of loving parents. Elaborating on his career or daily accomplishments was easy. Not once did I see him unwilling to field questions or fail to greet those mesmerized by his presence. Teasing the laws of the universe, he became a greater sum than that of the accumulated parts. Especially when one examined the big picture — aligning all the firsts — only then could one visualize the whole realm of the accomplishment. Rounded perfectly, the end was almost as great as the beginning.

Fortunately, his methods were proven and his dream came true. Interestingly, dreams start just like that, a simple vision. Next, they develop into a way of life. Depending on the support of the masses and the quality of the achievement, it becomes an everlasting celebration.

The description is correct. He conquered the iron and his fanfare will receive the time-tested bronze reward. Exercising the true humility of greatness provides a unique immortality.

Funny is the will of great men. Restless by nature. Undefeated at birth. Intrigued by mystery. Taunted by failure.

{DM}

Backword

As Americans we celebrate the symbolic movement of a rodent from winter darkness to anticipated spring light. As you re-read the collection, move away from shadow gray — into the light.

~*Duck Miller*

"Because it is there."

~*George Mallory*

About the Author

Duck Miller was born on a small farm and was raised by two blue-collar parents who toiled to secure the best possible education for all of their children. After graduating from a competitive liberal arts college, Duck began pursuing his version of the American Dream. He currently works promoting his writings and enjoys spending time outdoors. Recently, Miller has dabbled in decoy carving.

www.thewhistlepig.net

Sightings!
Have you seen his shadow?
Send us a picture of your
Whistle Pig sighting! View pictures
of where The Whistle Pig
is popping up at www.thewhistlepig.net

Follow the Hunt!
Get the latest news on the search for
Duck's key! Visit www.thewhistlepig.net

Send an Autographed Gift Copy!
The Whistle Pig is already wrapped
and waiting to be autographed
and shipped to your gift recipients.
Order online at www.thewhistlepig.net

Get Whistle Pig Stuff!
T-Shirts, hats, stickers, and more
available at www.thewhistlepig.net

Quantity discounts are available
for qualifying institutions.
Please contact the publisher at
publisher@canvasbackpress.com

Available to the trade from
all major wholesalers.

Available from your favorite
local bookstore.

For more information, visit
www.thewhistlepig.net

Spread the Rumor;
Get the Stuff!

Sport Cap

White cotton twill embroidered with the shadow of The Whistle Pig.

T-Shirt

White 100% cotton beefy tees screen printed with The Whistle Pig logo on the back.

2" Sticker

Use this 2" white outdoor vinyl sticker to leave your mark where you've been hunting Duck's key!

3" Window Cling

3" white static cling vinyl you can apply to any glass surface. Let 'em know yer a hunter!

Matchbooks

Pass the book and spread the fire! Functional book of matches that gets attention.